If The Shoe Fits

Written by

ALAN & SUZANNE OSMOND

Illustrated by

THOMAS AARRESTAD

A TWICE UPON A TIME TALE

Cinderella

Published by Ideals Children's Books
An imprint of Hambleton-Hill Publishing, Inc.
1501 County Hospital Road
Nashville, Tennessee 37218

Library of Congress Cataloging-in-Publication Data
Osmond, Alan
If the shoe fits / by Alan Osmond ; illustrated by Thomas Aarrestad.
p.   cm. -- (Twice uon a time)
Summary: Cinderella's son worries that his mean cousins will beat him in the King's Race, so the fairy godmother who helped his mother reappears with some assistance for him.
ISBN 1-57102-133-7 (hardcover)
[1. Characters in literature--Fiction. 2. Cousins--Fiction. 3. Running--Fiction.] I. Aarrestad, Thomas, ill.
II. Title. III. Series: Osmond, Alan. Twice upon a time.
PZ7.08345If   1998
[E]--dc21   98-19244
CIP
AC

First Edition

Written by Alan Osmond
Illustrated by Thomas Aarrestad

Cover and book design LaughlinStudio

ALAN & SUZANNE OSMOND

Suzanne and I dedicate this book to our eight sons:

Michael, Nathan, Douglas, David, Scott, Jon, Alex,

and Tyler. . .a.k.a. The Osmonds—Second Generation.

When telling our boys bedtime stories, the concept

came that the classics can also live on for

a second generation and could be told not only once,

but "Twice Upon A Time."

THOMAS AARRESTAD

To my Mother and Father.

Twice upon a Twice upon a time, in the castle where the legend of the glass slipper was born, there lived a young prince named James. He was the son of Queen Ella and the king, who were once known as Cinderella and Prince Charming.

Living in a cottage near the castle were Queen Ella's two step-sisters and their sons, Melvin and Marvin. They were always getting into trouble and playing tricks on their step-cousin, Prince James.

The boys all attended the Royal Academy Elementary School, where the Royal Field Day was coming up in less than a month. Since Prince James was so busy learning to be king, all he could do was watch from the window as his step-cousins practiced getting faster and faster.

One day, just a week before the race, Prince James asked his parents, "I know I have to work very hard to be king, but how can I win the King's Race at the Royal Field Day if all I do is study?"

Queen Ella knew how hard James worked at his studies. "In order to be good at something, you have to practice," she said. "Since your father is so busy, I will be your coach. Let's start by seeing how fast you can run around the entire castle!"

One day, Melvin and Marvin were hanging around the castle and laughing at the Prince while he practiced. They made fun of his shoes. They made fun of his running. And they made fun of his having his mother for a coach.

"You may be our next leader," Melvin said.

"But you'll be following us at the races!" finished Marvin.

Then they ran away, chanting, "Wiggle, wiggle, run, run. Beating you will sure be fun!"

With tears in his eyes, Prince James said to himself, "I'll show those cousins of mine. I'm going to win!"

The evening before the race, Queen Ella was saying goodnight to her son when suddenly, in a sparkle of fairy light, the Fairy Godmother appeared.

"Hello Ella," she said. "So nice to see you again!" She turned to the prince. "James," the Fairy Godmother said sweetly, "since you have worked so hard, I want to make sure that when you race tomorrow you are the most handsome young runner ever. Ella, would you please bring me the glass slippers and the gown you wore a long time ago at Prince Charming's ball?"

Queen Ella quickly ran to her room and brought back the items that the Fairy Godmother had asked for.

With a wave of her magic wand, the Fairy Godmother chanted, "Gown of gold satin, slippers of glass, let the Prince do his running with class!"

POOF! There before him were the most magnificent running suit and the coolest pair of running shoes ever seen! The Prince's eyes lit up as he thanked the Fairy Godmother.

But the prince's eyes weren't the only ones that were wide open! Melvin and Marvin were watching from outside the prince's window.

"Wow!" they whispered.

"There is something very important about these clothes that you must remember," said the Fairy Godmother.

Just then, Melvin slipped from the window and fell down, dragging Marvin with him to the ground.

"What did she say?" squealed Melvin. "What did the Fairy Godmother say?"

"I don't know! I can't hear anything from down here!" grunted Marvin. "But I do know we have to get those magic clothes or else tomorrow he will win the race and we will look like two big losers!"

13

While Prince James dreamed of winning the King's Race, Melvin and Marvin sneaked into his room. They took the suit and the shoes and off they ran!

The next morning, Prince James was shocked when he found his new clothes missing. He searched everywhere, but they were nowhere to be found. Fearing he would be late and miss the race, he put on his old outfit and hurried off to the school.

hen Prince James arrived, he spotted his cousins right away. Melvin was wearing his running suit! Marvin was wearing his cool running shoes!

Prince James was really angry, but before he could say anything, it was time to begin the games. All the way through the obstacle course Prince James ran, dodged, and jumped, giving everything he had to make the finals of the first event.

Up in the stands, the King noticed that something was wrong with his son. "Our son looks very discouraged, not like a future king at all!" he said.

"Those step-cousins have stolen James' new running clothes!" Ella said. "I must go speak to him before the next event." She walked down to the field.

"Oh Mother!" cried the Prince. "I can't win the race without my magical running suit and shoes." Prince James sat down on the field with his head in his hands.

"Forget those silly clothes! The only thing that matters is that you do your very best!" Queen Ella gave her son a big hug.

He looked up at her with a smile. "Thanks, Mom."

All morning long, Melvin and Marvin won race after race. The Prince never came in first, but he always tried as hard as he could. In the end, he was good enough to win a spot in the King's Race.

James took his place at the starting line.

"How do you like my new suit?" snickered Melvin.

"And how about my new shoes?" added Marvin. "No one can beat us now that we have these magic clothes."

Prince James didn't say a word or even look at his cousins. He just remembered what his mother had told him and stood ready to do his very best.

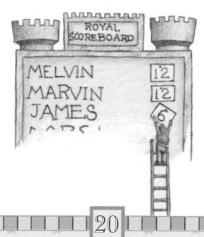

The race judge lifted his arm. "Ready. Set. Go!" The racers were off! First Melvin pulled ahead, and Marvin quickly caught up. Prince James was running faster than ever before, and for a moment he was in the lead.

"Why isn't my suit making me faster than Prince James?" wondered Melvin as sweat began to trickle down his face.

"What's wrong with these magic shoes?" thought Marvin as Prince James pulled along beside him.

As they neared the final lap, the old bell in the castle tower began to toll the noon hour. Just as Prince James was crossing the finish line ahead of his cousins, Melvin's suit disappeared in a poof of fairy dust, and tangled around his feet was the long skirt of a gold evening gown!

At the same time, Marvin lost his balance and went tumbling head over heels as his cool new running shoes turned back into Queen Ella's high-heeled glass slippers!

As everyone surrounded the prince to congratulate him on his victory, the Fairy Godmother walked over to Melvin and Marvin and asked, "Did somebody forget about the twelve o'clock rule?"

Everyone laughed at the sight of the two cousins, Melvin wearing the Queen's dress and Marvin wearing two glass slippers! James laughed so hard he could barely make it to the judges' stand to receive his medal.

At the celebration that evening, Melvin and Marvin went to Prince James and apologized for stealing his things. James forgave his cousins like a good future king should.

Queen Ella smiled proudly at her son and said, "Do you think these old shoes will still fit?" As she started to put one on, Prince James took it from her, kissed her cheek, and said, "Thank you, Mother, for believing in me."

The future king knelt and placed the slipper on Queen Ella's foot, just as his father had done long ago. It was a perfect fit, just as it had been once upon a time.

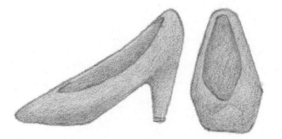

THE END